SNOW WHITE

MIRROR MIRROR, WHO IS SLUTTIEST OF THEM ALL

WRITTEN BY

JOHN JAYNESIS

Copyright © 2023 Discovery Stories rights reserved.

No part of this publication may be reproduced, distributed, or transmitted in any form or by any means, including photocopying, recording, or other electronic or mechanical methods, without the prior written permission of the publisher, except in the case of brief quotations embodied in reviews and certain other non-commercial uses permitted by copyright law.

ISBN: 9798395934857

ISBN-13: 979-8395934857

CONTENTS

CHAPTER 1 9

CHAPTER 2 21

CHAPTER 3 47

CHAPTER 4 63

CHAPTER 5 95

AUTHOR NOTE 127

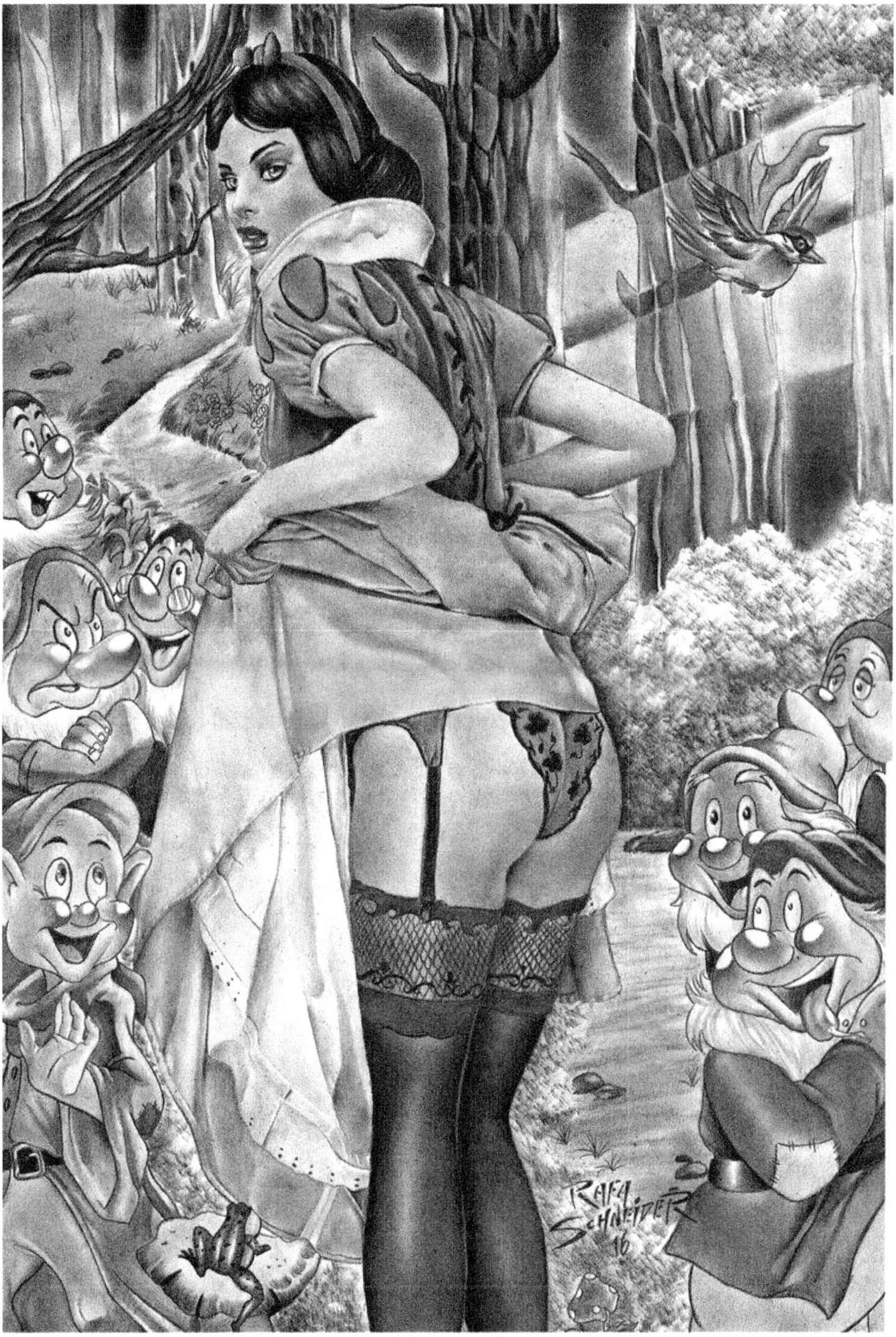
RAFA SCHNEIDER 16

CHAPTER 1

"Mirror, Mirror on the wall, who is the Fairest One of all?" commands the Queen. She stands adorned in raiment of gold, her dark hair graced with a silver crown, her skin pale, her lips full and lustrous – her beauty glorious and, surely, unsurpassable.

"Fair art thou, O Queen," replies the Mirror, "and thy dark hair, thy pale skin, and thy full red lips are things of great beauty. But yet, show me more, Majesty, that I might tell whether thou art truly the Fairest in the Land." The Queen smiles knowingly, letting her robes fall gracefully to her waist, revealing her full breasts, firm and luscious as ripe melons.

"O, fair art thou, O Queen," gasps the Mirror in delight. "Thy dark hair, thy pale skin, and thy full red lips are things of beauty; and yea, thy tits are gorgeous, suckable, fuckable marvels – surely the fairest in the Kingdom and beyond. But yet, reveal more to me, Majesty: let me see thy tight cunt, that I might say whether or not thy beauty is truly unsurpassed."

The Queen knows this routine, and she smirks as she lets her robes drop to the floor, revealing her bald pussy, pink and glistening, its soft dangling lips shining with nectar.

The Mirror moans in pleasure. "Fair art thou, O Queen – O fuck: thy hair, thy skin, thy lips, thy huge bulging tits, and now thy tasty dripping Queenly Quim, are surely the most wondrous in the Land. Slide thy fingers into that hot cunt and taste thy Sovereign Savour, that thy Servant may revel in the glory of thy Beauteous Body."

The Queen does so, and soon her fingers are webbed with the finest filigree of cunt-slime, which she licks off with outstretched tongue, glorying in her inimitable pungent royal sweetness. The Magic Mirror groans in pleasure: "Fuck yea, O Quimful Queen, that is truly the most Perfect Pussy in the whole Kingdom, nay, throughout the Seven Kingdoms of this Continent – guaranteed to make each man or woman swoon, prostrate himself at thy feet, and worship thy Courtly Cuntness, thy

Victorious Vulva. But yet, thou hast not yet revealed to me thy Perfect Posterior which – though surely a thing of beauty, may yet – who knows? – be surpassed by someone else."

"Ha!" The Queen laughs with derision. "Who could surpass my arse, Mirror Minion? If I have more beautiful hair, skin, lips, tits and cunt than any other in all Europe, then my arse is surely my crowning glory: curvaceous, tight, slappable, lickable, pungent and fuckable – who can improve upon this?" She twirls round to reveal her bottom – and, yea, it is a marvel to behold.

The Mirror groans with pleasure and desire: "Oh fuck, oh yea, oh Motherfucking Miraculous Majesty, show me that hot fucking arse, squeeze it, spank it, jiggle it, twerk it. O yes, O Queen, thine is surely the most Beauteous Bottom in the Land!"

The Queen laughs triumphantly. "And so, my Lascivious Lookingglass, my Wanking Windowpane – wilt thou at last declare thy Queen the Fucking Fairest in the Land?"

"Ah – but yet, one thing remains to be investigated, O Marvellous Motherfucking Majesty, before I can declare thee Vaginally Victorious among all women. Come closer, that I may better investigate that Royal Rectum, that Chivalrous Shitter, which winketh wankily at me from between thy Basilic Buttcheeks. For it is in the Domineering Depths of thy Sovereign

Stinkhole that true beauty will ever be revealed."

The Queen shifts her bottom backwards, till her soft cheeks are pressed up against the warm surface of the Mirror, and she feels her anus winking cheekily against the glass. "O fuck, O yea, O behold, O fuck ye fuck ye," groans the Mirror in pleasurable ecstasy. The Queen feels something soft, wet and flexible caressing her brown hole, hears the Mirror slurping and slobbering as it casts all decorum to one side and moans in anilingual ecstasy: "O shit, O fuck, O scrummy cunting arsehole, O yea, O let me eat thy fucking arse, O Queen, let me plunge my Tricksome Tongue deep in that filthy fucking shithole."

"My Motherfucking Minion, my Butteating

Bondsman," replies the Queen, "stick thy finger in there, do! Pinky-penetrate my Paramount Pungent Posterior!"

"FUCK YEAAAA!" yells the Mirror in lustful desperation. "Feel me finger-fuck that Filthy Fundament, Majesty! Not just one, not two, but three invisible Fucking Fingers in that Regal Rectum, that thy August Anus may gape O-glorious for my pleasure!"

"FUUUUUCK!" screams the Queen in delight, as she feels her posterior penetrated by three twirling curling unseen digits. Her own hand furiously rubs her Courtly Clit, edging herself closer and closer to her climax, as she screams: "Now plunge thy prick into my Royal Rectum, make me come over thy Fucking Fenestration. Go on, Mirror, ram that Fiefly Fuckstick in and out of my cunted shithole, split me in two with thy Peasant Prick, thy Captive Cock!"

Immediately the Queen feels something huge and stiff pressing against her butthole – followed by the punch, the scrape, the squeeze of the Mirrorly Manhood filling her up. "FUCK YEA!" she screams. "Squirt all thy cream deep in my Domineering Dirtpipe, Motherfucking Mirror. Fucking drown me in Servile Semen whilst I come all over thy Magic Manhood. And then tell me that I am the Fucking Fairest in the Land!"

The Mirror continues to mercilessly pound his prick

in and out of the royal anus. "FAIR ART THOU, O FUCKING QUEEN!" he bellows in ecstasy. "Thy hair is black as ebony, thy skin as white as snow, thy lips as red as the red red rose, thy cunt as pink as hyacinth, thy arse as sq ueezable and fuckable as any throughout the Continent and beyond." The Queen feels her arse pounded harder, faster, deeper, as the Mirror continues: "But yet there is one who surpasseth thee – for her arsehole is fairer than thine: its savour is sweeter, its taste more tempting, its grip tighter, its gape wider, its rim smoother, O wretched Queen, than thine own August Arsehole."

"WHAT?!" screeches the Queen. "Who is the one whose Butthole Beauty exceeds mine? Who dares to challenge the Royal Rectum?"

"SNOOOW WHIIITE!" bellows the Mirror, as he climaxes copiously as only a Magic Mirror can. The Queen feels the Mirror's semen spray-paint her interior, splashing wildly against her rectal walls. She feels the invisible manhood withdraw, yet continue to squirt its cream across her buttocks and up her back. Cum drips out of her arsehole, courses down her dangling cunt-lips, dribbles down her thighs, pools behind her heels, and seeps magically across the marble floor. "Snow White is now sixteen, O Queen," pants the Mirror, "and her tight teenage arsehole is now the Fairest in the Land! Thy Buttock Beauty is supplanted, Majesty."

"LIAR!!!" screams the Queen, wheeling round, but

losing her balance in the slippery semen and falling face-first in the pool of cum, her crown tipping off her head and landing with a splash. Fuck-cream flows across the marble floor, rendering her helplessly prone, blubbing and glubbing, cum-faced and frustrated. "GUARDS! ARREST THIS MIRROR!!" she screeches. Her guards come running, but can manage nothing more than to slip and slide across the semen-coated floor, ending up in a cum-spattered jumble against the wall.

"INGRATE! TRAITOR! ASSASSIN!" screams the Queen at her once-faithful Mirror. "I AM THE FAIREST IN THE LAND! AND MY ARSEHOLE IS THE MOST BEAUTIFUL THE WORLD HAS EVER SEEN!" As if to prove it, she pulls herself up onto her hands and knees, emits a long loud squelchy fart from her fucked-out anus, before slipping and collapsing again face-first on the cum-soaked marble floor.

"SNOW WHITE SHALL DIE!!!"

CHAPTER 2

"I say, why did Her Majesty send you with me today?" asks Snow White. She is indeed fair of face, with hair black as ebony, skin white as snow, and lips red as the rose. Her dress is pastel blue, and her smile and her laughter light up the forest glade. Her voice is pinched and nasal, in the best tradition of Anna Neagle, Pathé newsreels, Hello Children Everywhere – and the finest of royal princesses. A stream babbles through the clearing, ending in a small pond of clear blue water, still but for the occasional ripple caused by the flick of a fish tail.

The young Huntsman tries to appear unfazed by the q uestion – but lying does not come easily to him.

"She wants me to protect ye, to keep ye safe," he says awkwardly, looking at his feet.

"You don't say! Is that why you are carrying that huge axe?" replies the girl. (She pronounces "axe" a bit like "ex" – just as a princess should.) "To chop awff the head of anyone who threatens me?" She giggles artlessly, twirling her body, her arms outstretched so her skirt flares like a flower, her smooth face dappled by the sun shining through the leaves.

The Huntsman tries to chuckle with her. He is strong, young and handsome, captivated by the girl's beauty, and dreading his assigned task. "By yer leave, ma'am, I'll just go over the other side of that rise for a minute," he blurts, "and check out the surroundings."

"I say, shouldn't you be staying here with me? You are supposed to be 'protecting' me, aren't you?" giggles Snow White. She twirls a lock of her dark hair absent-mindedly.

"I won't be long, yer 'Ighness," says the Huntsman, as he turns, frowning, and heads up a slope away from the glade.

"Toodle-pip," calls the Princess, before giggling to herself, once the Huntsman is out of sight, "I'll have to be jolly quick then, won't I?" She lies down on a daffodil-strewn grassy mound and begins to sing – a sweet appoggiatura-laden soprano dominant seventh which echoes invitingly through the forest.

Her friends duly begin to gather: a flock of sparrows, a bevy of rabbits, a dray of squirrels, two young deer, a flight of sparrows – and a turtle. They form an affectionate circle around her, as she hitches up her skirt to reveal her soft thatch of pubic hair carefully trimmed into a dark triangle pointing the way to her tight pubescent pussy.

"Well, old chums, what of it, eh?" sq ueaks the girl. "I am all of sixteen now, and still a virgin! Shall I prove it you?" she giggles.

The deer nod solemnly, the rabbits and sq uirrels gambol about, and the birds chatter and chirp as they perch on the branches of a silver birch, looking down in expectation. The turtle watches studiously, as the girl licks her fingers and begins to gently lubricate her outer lips.

"You see," explains Snow White, "these are my labia maiora. Sounds jolly important, doesn't it – very High Church, don't you think? Gratias agimus tibi propter labia maiora tua!" she intones in mock ecclesiastical tones. "Not at all difficult prising these apart: see how soft and puffy they are? That's because I'm already feeling just a tiny bit excited! Soon they'll be all swollen and pink!" She titters with delight, and her friends follow suit, chirping and chattering where they perch.

"But these," continues the girl, "are my labia minora

– and that's something quite different entirely, because inside them is hiding this little flap of skin – see?" She stretches her inner lips wide to show off her intact hymen. "I say, do you realise" – Snow White licks her fingers again, slathering a large smear of saliva across her vulva – "that is what makes me a virgin: because no one has ever fucked my pussy before – isn't that utterly champion?!" She giggles again – and her friends follow suit. "I know that doesn't mean an awful lot to you – I mean, you rabbits are always at it like rabbits, aren't you?" (The rabbits look sheepish.) "But for humans, especially for royalty like me, being a virgin is terribly important! No one is permitted to penetrate this pussy until I am properly married." (She pronounces the word rather like "merried" – as a well brought-up

Princess should.) "But then," she continues, "my husband can stick his big hard cock in there, rupture my hymen, fill me up with his hot cum, and we will all live happily ever after – isn't that simply spiffing!" She claps her hands in self-congratulation, and her menagerie of admirers hoot and chatter in appreciation.

Just over the rise, the Huntsman is spying out the lie of the land. The sky is clear, and he can see down the other side of the hill to where the Great Forest lies, wild and untamed. In the far distance, beyond the woods, there shine the glinting marbled towers of the Great City in the Far Kingdom. "There she could be safe," he mutters to himself. "If I let 'er go, she could live."

The choice is easily made. He remembers his childhood, growing up a servant in the King's household, admiring the Princess – a mere four years younger than he – from afar. As a child, so pretty and delightful; as a teenager sweet and elegant and graceful, even when her father the gracious King died and her foul stepmother became Queen. Even when all hope has been wrung out of the Kingdom, Snow White continues to exude light and life. "She must live," resolves the young Huntsman, "for she is the only 'ope our Land 'as. And I could not bear to kill 'er," he sighs. With that, he abandons his axe on the grass of the hilltop and turns back towards the glade.

As he descends the slope, he hears the sound of

singing, giggling and chattering. "Talking to herself and her forest friends, as usual," he presumes. But as he approaches, he sees that things are not quite as usual as he imagined, for the Princess is reclining on a grassy mound, surrounded by daffodils, her long skirt hitched up to her waist, fingering her clitoris as she sings to her forest friends:

Someday my Prince will come…

before giggling, "Hee hee! 'will come' – get it? 'will come'!" He laughter tinkles carillon-like though the forest.

"But," continues the girl, "until I am merried and my husband gets to smesh my hymen to smithereens, I have to sadly make do with other forms of pleasure – isn't that just beastly?" Her animal friends nod sagely, as the eavesdropping Huntsman's penis begins to rise in his trousers. He can just see Snow White through the trees, and conceals himself behind a large oak to watch.

"So," continues Snow White, "instead of sticking things in my pussy, I stroke my clit! See this little button here? If I rub it, it gets all swollen, and starts to feel jolly nice, I must say. Have a look, do!" Her friends nod again, as Snow White hawks a large gob of spit onto her clitoris and begins to rub it with a broad circular motion, until little sq ueaks of pleasure begin to emanate from her lips.

The Huntsman has his penis out now, and is slowly stroking it as he watches in rapt attention, thumb and two fingers of his right hand gently pulling his damp foreskin back and forth along his glans, whilst his left palm caresses his heavy testicles. "|I say," says Snow White to her friends, "I think it looks jolly pretty when I rub my clit, don't you? Because then one can see right into my pussy, without anything in the way. And one can watch it going all sq uishy and bubbly – isn't that capital?" They chatter and chirp their approval.

"What about you, Mister Huntsman?" calls Snow White. "Don't you think it's jolly pretty too?!"

The Huntsman, behind his oak, freezes in horror,

and his penis goes suddenly soft in his hand. He thought himself hidden, and now frantically tries to conceal himself yet more, desperately crouching down behind a bush and wincing as a thorn grazes his penis. Snow White giggles, "Silly chap! I can see you reflected in that pond. Are you watching me stroke my pussy? Does that make your cock terribly stiff?"

Torn between lust and terror, the young Huntsman does not know how to react. Flee? But then what about the Princess, so beautiful, so lovely, whom he has decided to save? And besides, her pussy shines and beckons with irresistible pubescent glory. His shaft starts to go hard again.

"Oh, do come out of there, Mister Huntsman, there's a good chap!" calls Snow White. "No point in hiding now, what!" Trembling, he steps out into the glade and stands before his mistress, his stiff shaft throbbing and eager, his glans glistening with pre-cum. "I'm so sorry, ma'am," he mutters half-heartedly.

"Oh look!" squeals the Princess, ignoring his apologetic air. "What a big cock you have, Huntsman! Well, bigger than Father's was at any rate. Come closer, do – let me see, spit spot!" She beckons peremptorily.

The Huntsman waddles forward, his trousers bunched around his shins, his stiff penis waggling from side to side. The Princess giggles and claps her approval, as her circle of forest friends parts to allow the young man to approach. "What is your name, Huntsman?" asks Snow White, as she continues to absent-mindedly rub her vulva, three fingers gently sq uelching into the wet space between her outer pussy-lips. "I remember you from when I was little, lurking in the background in the Palace courtyard, watching me play. Your father was the King's Chief Steward once, wasn't he? What do they call you?"

"Callum, Yer 'Ighness," replies the Huntsman. His penis is still hard, and he cannot take his eyes off the girl's pussy – glistening, soft, sq uidgy, pink.

Show White bursts into peals of laughter. "Callum?!

You are joking, aren't you? Please say you're joking, 'Callum the Cuntsman'! Are you a 'Cuntsman', Callum?" she teases.

Callum the Huntsman mutters indistinctly. He is shocked, humiliated, at a loss for words, yet transfixed by the sight of the Princess's young vulva glowing up at him, squelching and dripping as her fingers continue to gently massage her pussy-lips. "Yes, Yer 'Ighness…" he nods.

"Jolly good, Callum the Cuntsman! Come and have a closer look at this cunt then, do!" But then the Princess pauses. "Oh, I see," she muses out loud, "you're shocked by my language – a bit infra dig, is that it?"

Callum the Cuntsman is panting and trembling, but speechless – appalled by the behaviour of his mistress, yet entranced by her beauty. Helpless at the sight of Snow White's glistening pink cunt, now stretched wide by her delicate fingers, its heady scent mixing with the perfume of wildflowers and heather, the Huntsman's cock is tumescent and desperate, and he cannot help but resume stroking it with his broad palm.

"Well, I can't say I blame you, Master Cuntsman," continues the Princess, unperturbed. "I too was shocked when I first heard words like that, don't you know. It was in the Palace kitchens late at night, and I overheard Annie the scullery maid talking to Sir

John de Thomas, Captain of the Palace Guard. I don't think they knew I was listening, but Annie was talking in her lovely rustic accent, saying things like, 'Ye loike moy cunt, Johnny? Ye wanna fuck it?' She speaks like that, you see," explains Snow White, before giggling again with feigned innocence: "Well, I declare, I didn't even know what a 'cunt' was at the time, much less how to 'fuck' one! So I peered round the corner, and there they were, by candlelight – she leaning back against the counter, and he plunging his cock in and out of her! (I know!) And well, it was so jolly lovely to watch, and 'cunt' just seemed just the perfect word for such a pretty thing. But then the girl said – in her rustic accent, naturally, so you must forgive me if I don't get it quite right, 'Now fuck moy arrse, Johnny, good 'n' 'arrd!' Now I didn't know that it was even possible to fuck one's 'arrse'! But she turned round and leant over, and the chap did just that – imagine! And so I decided then and there that someone would do that to me someday! Isn't that awfully jolly!?"

Callum's heart pounds, and his cock jerks in his palm, at the sound of his Princess's wide-eyed descent into such deliciously plebeian language. Snow White grins, and ups the ante, switching – whether deliberately or unconsciously Callum cannot tell, and does not care – into a broad West Country accent: "See, Callum, my cunt is gettin' all juicy as I rub it. I can't let ye fuck it – because we arren't married, and besoides, I really ought to marry a Prince, not a 'Cuntsman'," she giggles. "But go on, stroke tha' big stiff cock for me, Master Callum, while I rub my 'ot fuckin' cunt!" The Princess is rubbing the palm of one hand over and around her wet vulva now, making her fuck-lips squelch noisily at her touch, whilst the other hand pounds her clitoris. "See 'ow moy cunt is all juicy an' wet an' pink? I bet ye want to fuck it, don't you? I bet ye want to ram that 'uge fuckin' cock deep in moy cunt, split me aparrt with yer 'ot rod, fill me up with yer creamy fuckin' cum. Do ye loike 'ow I'm speakin' to you, Callum – tell me!"

"Oh yes, Your 'Ighness, yes!" pants Callum the Cuntsman, revelling in the sensory overload of his mistress' ongoing filthy monologue.

"Good, Callum!" moans the girl in delight. "Now,

'ere's a special treat for ye, Callum: watch me stick a finger up moy arrse – look!" The Princess lifts her buttocks upwards so that her Huntsman can see her brown puckered hole winking at him, before wetting it with her saliva and sliding the middle finger of her right hand into it two knuckles deep. "Oh fuck, tha' 's good, Callum – now watch me make it two fingerrs, Masterr Cuntsman – and then three! And then let me show ye what Annie did next: she let the Captain of the Guarrd ram 'is 'ole fuckin' cock deep insoide 'er arrse, so 'is balls slapped against 'er cunt-lips – and then, when 'e pulled it out it was all gapin' loike a fuckin' cavern – JUST LOIKE THIS!" Princess Snow White slides two fingers of each hand into her anus from each side, pulling it wide open with both hands so that Callum can gaze deep into her gaping rectum.

"Ye loike that, Misterr Cuntsman? Ye loike lookin' deep insoide moy royal arrse?" She throws back her head and laughs with untrammelled delight.

Callum blubbers and groans stupidly, as his fist pounds harder and faster up and down his stiff throbbing shaft. "Will you come with me, Mister Cuntsman?" continues the Princess. "Go on, jerk all that 'ot fuckin' cum out, all over moy pretty Princess arrse, whoile I play with moy cunt!" Callum stumbles forward, jerking his cock rapidly in his fist, as he feels his jism rising through his thick shaft. Standing before Snow White, he roars in ecstasy as his cock-cream spurts out of his glans and showers down over his mistress's pretty pale buttocks, splattering generously into her winking brown hole.

"OH YEA FUUUCK!" screams the Princess, as she feels her Cuntsman's warm jizz spatter over her. "COME ALL OVER MOY PRETTY PRINCESS ARRSE, CUNTSMAN! MAKE ME LOOK LOIKE A FUCKIN' SCULLERY MAID!" She thrashes and sq ueals as her own cunt spasms at her own touch, her forest friends cheering and screeching in delight. She scoops the man-cum up with her left hand and licks it, savouring the pungent salty taste, as she mutters and moans, "Oh, lovely filthy cum, all over moy scullery maid arrse…"

Callum's cock dangles flaccid now, and he stands sheepishly, terrified at what might happen next. But Snow White giggles and lowers her buttocks to the forest floor, before smearing her right hand over her cunt one last time and raising it up towards the Huntsman, fingers twirling seductively. "Have a taste of the royal labia maiora, Master Callum," she instructs, in her now-regained customary royal accent. "After all, you are my Cuntsman, aren't you?" Callum leans forward and gingerly licks the tips of Snow White's fingers, tasting the heavenly flavour. "Deeper, Callum, deeper," encourages the Princess, pushing three fingers into his mouth. "Lick it all up, Cuntsman, all this juice is for you, my cunting commoner…"

Callum sucks and slobbers, relishing the heady stink. "Yer 'Ighness," he attempts to speak, despite the flavoured fist in his mouth, "ye must fwee forfwiv. 'Er

Majesty wantf you dead; she fent me to kill ye. Ye must fwee acwoff the Gweat Forest to the Far Kingdom, where ye will be fafe!" A dribble of pungent saliva escapes his lips, as the Princess withdraws the royal hand from his mouth. "Flee, my mistress, flee!"

The Princess regards her Huntsman with astonishment. "What? The Queen? It cannot be! Why?"

"She fears you more fair than she," replies Callum.

"But ... but – which way? I do not know the way!" she cries.

"Over that rise, and due east, till you reach the other

side of the Forest!" urges the Huntsman, his large but flaccid penis still dangling from his fly.

The Princess rises to her feet. "Can you lead me, my dear old chums?" she asks of her animal friends.

The animals nod enthusiastically, and lead the way swiftly toward the rise beyond which lies the border of the Kingdom and the beginning of the Great Forest. Snow White follows, but turns at the top of the hill to call: "Callum the Cuntsman, I salute you! I will think of you awften, and will always remember your service with gratitude! Someday, when this Land is free again, I will reward you! My cunt is destined for the Prince I merry, but I swear to you, my Royal Cuntsman, that the next time we meet, you may fuck the Royal Arse!" She grins, laughs, turns, and disappears from sight.

Callum stands, stunned, his flaccid penis still dripping cum onto the daffodils, a grin on his face, but a tear in his eye as he gazes after his beloved Princess. "God save ye, Princess Snow White," he mutters, before turning and wending his way back towards the Palace, buttoning up his fly as he goes.

CHAPTER 3

Snow White walks swiftly, escorted through the Forest by her animal friends. Tears run down her face now, as she realises the sheer horror of her situation. "The Queen wants me dead! Oh, how utterly awful! So, to the Far Kingdom must I escape. But then what? And who will take care of me now?"

She walks, and as she walks her friends bring her sustenance – berries and nuts and wild fruits – and guide her to springs of cool water where she may slake her thirst. But as darkness begins to fall, and there is no sign of reaching the other side of the Forest, let alone the Far Kingdom, she asks, "But where, O dear chums, can I spend the night? I am not like you, used to sleeping under the stars. I am a Princess, and must have a bed for the night, don't you know?"

The animals confer briefly, chattering and hooting in heated deliberation, before leading the Princess off the main path at an angle, over a rise and down a steep incline, into a clearing with a stream running through it and, over the other side of a low footbridge, a small, thatched oak-beamed cottage.

It is dusk now, and the light is failing fast. "Who lives here?" asks the Princess. "And is it safe?" The animals seem to shrug their shoulders, shifting awkwardly from foot to foot – but Snow White's question is answered forthwith, as the front door of the house opens, and a small light appears floating in the doorway. The light floats down the garden path towards Snow White and her friends, at about the height of the Princess' eyes, all the while glowing with a strange magical purple hue. It stands vertically, about eight inches long and thick as Snow White's slender wrist. As it approaches it become clear what it is.

"Oh I say!" exclaims Snow White. "It's a Dildo! A Magic Dildo! How awfully jolly!"

The purple floating luminous Dildo throbs and pulsates with a magic internal light. It appears to bow, and then beckon. As Snow White follows, more floating shining Dildos appear at the doorway to the

Cottage – seven of them in total, all colours of the rainbow, glimmering and pulsating seductively.

"Ohhh!" sighs the Princess. "I'm sure I will be very comfortable here!" She steps over the threshold into the Cottage, escorted by the Seven Dildos, and gently shuts the door behind her.

"FILL THAT FUCKING FUNDAMENT, MIRROR MINION! REAM MY ROYAL RECTUM!" screeches the Queen. She is on her hands and knees on the marble floor, her bottom pressed hard against the steamy surface of her Mirror, as she feels his invisible Magic Manhood pound mercilessly in and out of her anus. "Cum in my fucking filth-pot and tell me I am the Fairest of Them All! For Snow White is dead, her heart excised by my faithful Royal Huntsman. Now there is none to challenge me!"

"If thou wouldst have me proclaim thee Fairest in the Land, O Quimly Queen," pants the Mirror, "then let me see thee with all my Mirrorly Milt over thy Fair Fucking Face. Thy hair may be dark, thy skin pale, thy lips rouge – and, naturally, thy Courtly Cunt and August Arsehole unsurpassed – but, what if covered in cum, O Motherfucking Majesty? Will thy cream-covered features prove a Visage Victorious or Vile, a Face Fair or Foul?"

"Then sq uirt your Judgment of Jizz all over my Fucking Features, my Masturbating Minion," calls the Queen, whirling round and lifting her face in luminous anticipation, "and thou shalt surely see that Cum-Covered I am yet fairer than any in the Land. Watch thy Windowpane Wanksnot decorate me, see thy Enchanted Effluent embellish me, make me fairer still fuck-slimed than ever befoaaargh..." Her eyes shut but trembling in ecstatic expectation, she opens her mouth wide, her tongue extended and drooling, panting like a bitch on heat.

"THEN TAKE THIS, YOUR WHORISH HIGHNESS!" bellows the Mirror, as his cum squirts powerfully from his invisible member. The Queen feels the first few spurts land on her tongue, and moans in pleasure as she tastes the salty seed. Like pungent chlorinated cream, it fills her mouth until it overflows, dribbling down her chin and dripping onto her full breasts. She closes her mouth and swallows, feeling the mouthful of warm mirror-cum caress its way down her throat.

But the Mirror has not finished, of course, and continues to splatter magic gloop over the royal visage. "OH FUCK!" screams the Queen, as she feels multiple spurts of semen cover her face and hair, gluing her eyes shut, forming great rivulets down her forehead, cheeks and nose. Now glubbing and choking on the surfeit of fucksauce covering her face and filling her mouth, she screeches, "BEHOLD, MY SORCERER SERF, MY WANKING WINDOWPANE! See how fair is thy Queen when drowned in dick-juice, covered in cock-sauce, submerged in semen! Does not thy jism adorn me perfectly? Am I not the

Fairest Fuck-Face in the Land?"

"Fair art thou, O Motherfucking Majesty!" proclaims the Mirror, as his cum continues to splatter over his mistress, cascading down her breasts, stomach and crotch, to form a large slippery puddle which spreads over the marble floor. "Thy hair, thy skin, thy lips, thy tits, thy cunt, yea thine arse are fairer and more fuckable than near any in the Whole Wide World. But thou art deceived, O Majesty, for Snow White liveth still! And whether pristine of face or covered with cum, she still surpasseth thee in beauty, O wretched cum-soaked Queen."

"WHAT!" screeches the Queen. "Snow White still alive? Prove it, O Motherfucking Mirror! Hath my

Huntsman deceived me? Yea verily must he be executed at dawn! GUARDS!!!"

The guards come running, but once again slip and slide in the cum-pond which now fills the chamber, ending up in a tangled pile in the corner. The Queen ignores them, as the Mirror clouds over, steams up, and then displays a scene to prove the veracity of his tale. "See, O Whorish Highness – Snow White!"

The Queen gasps in shock, as she sees in the Mirror the likeness of the Princess – hair black as ebony, skin white as snow, lips red as the rose – but only just recognisable, for she is on her back, naked, buttocks raised and legs spread wide, her hair dishevelled, her eyes watering, her skin flushed, screaming at the top of her lungs, "I SAY, FUCK ME, DON'T YOU KNOW!!!"

"Behold, O Motherfucking Majesty," confirms the Mirror. "Snow White liveth. In the Cottage of the Seven Dildos, deep in the Great Forest, doth she make her abode. See – they fuck her now, in her arse and her face – but not her cunt, for yet doth she reserve that for her Prince."

Seven flying glowing Magic Dildos do indeed grace the scene. One, shining bright yellow, with a mind of its own, slides contentedly between Snow White's full breasts, its head pulsating with pleasure, slowly leaking lubricant to ease its passage. Two more, red and orange in colour, pound alternately in and out of the Princess' gaping arsehole, their russet glow illuminating the maroon beauty of her rectal cavity. "OH FUCK MY ARSE, DO, MY FINE SPIFFING DILDO CH–AAARGH!" sq ueals the Princess, as two more Dildos, glowing green and blue, force themselves simultaneously into her mouth, gagging her and making a geyser of throat-slime erupt from her face.

The Queen watches in horror and fascination, as the final two Magic Dildos, large and thick, dark blue and purple in hue, glide downwards through the air and begin nudging at Snow White's tight cunt-lips. "NOOO!" shouts Snow White, as best as she can with two Dildos gagging her throat, "NO' 'I MY CUNT! VAT'F FOR MY PWINCE, WHEN WE ARE

MEWWIED! 'UM ALL OVER ME INFTEAD!!!"

The Dildos kindly comply, gliding upwards, their shining indigo and violet cockheads throbbing in anticipation, before angling themselves down towards the Princess and then exploding, showering her face and hair with thick creamy cum. The yellow Dildo releases its cream too, sq uirting copiously over her full tits and bulging nipples, thick cum-streams flowing between her breasts and down her abdomen towards her clitoris. The green and blue Dildos explode in Snow White's mouth, filling her oral cavity with dildo-semen which overflows down her chin as she gags and splutters helplessly. Finally, the Princess' gaping rectum becomes the recipient of the red and orange Dildos' seed, filling with thick gloop until it too overflows, and pungent arse-flavoured jizz pours out and onto the ground.

"O God!" whimpers the Queen. "She is indeed beautiful! And still more fair covered in cum!"

It is true. Snow White is coated from the top of her beautiful head of black hair down to her thighs. Large globules of semen hang from her delicate features, and from her stiff nipples. Pools of cum have formed between her breasts, at her belly-button, in her cunt-cleft, and all the way down her crotch toward her arsehole. And when she smiles, her jizz-coated rose-red lips, illuminated by the multiple shining hues of the Seven Dildos, sparkle with such peaches-and-cream beauty as the world rarely sees. Spunk-soaked

Snow White is truly the Fairest in the Land.

"Bitch!" mutters the Queen. "Filthy tight-cunted cum-soaked whore! She shall pay for this! Mirror!!!"

The scene in the Mirror fades away, as the Mirror intones, "Now how may I serve thee, O Quimly Queen?"

The cum-soaked Queen stands, jizz dripping slowly down her naked body as she addresses her glass servant: "Give me Magic, O Mirror, to destroy Snow White once and for all!"

"Such Magic I do not know, O Whoring Highness. But I can teach thee Magic which will cast Snow

White into a deep sleep, from which she will ne'er awake. Then shalt thou be truly the Fairest in the Land."

"Never awake? Is there no way to break the spell?" demands the Queen.

The Mirror utters a derisory laugh. "One – but it shall never come to pass, Motherfucking Majesty. For only True Love's Arsefuck the spell shall break! And no man can fuck arse with True Love. For men are fickle, pleasure-driven, selfish and power-hungry creatures. A man may perchance kiss a woman out of True Love. Perhaps, occasionally, he may fuck her cunt with a similar sentiment. But when a man fucks arsehole, it is purely for his own perverted pleasure, for he desires nothing more than to treat the fairer sex as dirt, as slave, as whore, as confirmation of his own filth-ridden mind. No man will ever fuck Snow White's shit-slot out of True Love, but only out of untrammelled Lust. Fear not, Whoresome Highness: Snow White shall ever sleep."

The Queen listens intently to the Mirror's monologue, then smiles – the demented self-obsessed smile of one for whom only her own victory matters. "So teach me this Magic, my Marvellous Minion," she cackles. "For then will I be Fairest in the Land!"

CHAPTER 4

Callum the Huntsman sits by his hearth, brooding. Through his cabin window, in the distance, the gilded towers and turrets of the Royal Palace rise gleaming, their flags fluttering in the warm spring breeze. From the stone walls and oak rafters of his cabin hang the tools of his trade: bows and arrows, axes and knives, skins and heads of deer and rabbits.

Callum broods. And the object of his contemplation is Snow White. Since he waved her off towards the Great Forest, he has been unable to forget her. In his mind's eye he sees her smile, gracious and winning, filling the space with light and joy: helplessly, he smiles back at his imagined Princess, before reality intrudes on his fantasy and pulls him back to the present. "Damn," he mutters. "Will ye be all right, Princess?"

Soon he is remembering again the more carefree times, before the good King died and his evil widow came to the Throne. He remembers watching from the edge of the Palace courtyard as the Princess played in the gardens, fashioning daisy chains on the lawn, playing pooh-sticks on the bridge, giggling and laughing and singing with her animal friends as they chattered and chirruped around her. He had so wanted to join her, to hear her funny priggish royal voice speak to him, ask him to join in. He imagines her sq ueaking at him, "I say, young man, would you mind awfully fetching me that stick from the stream, there's a good fellow…" But that could never have been, for, as she never tired of singing, someday her Prince would come. And a mere Palace servant such as he must accept his lot in life.

But now he remembers her at their last encounter, on a daffodil-strewn hillock in the woods, grinning cheekily at him as her pink virgin cunt gleamed and glistened, her fingers sq uelching into that warm bubbling space between her outer lips, her intact maidenhood teasing, stretching, tantalising. Mindlessly, Callum pops open the buttons on his trousers and releases his penis – already stiff and throbbing at the thought of the lovely Princess. "Oh, Snow White," he moans, as he begins to stroke his shaft, slowly but firmly, and the image of her glistening cunt continues to fill his mind's eye. And then he remembers her anus, stretched open by her delicate fingers into a gorgeous gape, the sunlight glimmering off the interior of her rectal cavity, as her pinched royal voice calls out, "I swear to you, my Royal Cuntsman, that the next time we meet, you may fuck the Royal Arse!"

"Fuck the Royal Arse," echoes Callum to himself under his breath, "fuck the Royal Arse – oh Princess, you are joy and light and beauty! Forgive me..." His cock explodes, semen squirting desperately from his glans and spattering over his deerskin rug.

He surveys the mess, dissatisfied. That was pleasurable, to be sure, he thinks to himself, but not so pleasurable as to compensate for the lack of her. "God, keep her safe!" he mutters. "And may the time come when this accursed Queen is gone, and Snow White can render goodness and joy to this Kingdom once more..."

"Someday my Prince will come, " warbles Snow White, as she stands at the sink in her Cottage washing up. It is a fine sunny morning, and her forest friends are gathered at the kitchen window to hear her sing and chat, and to admire her winsome beauty.

"What fun I am having here!" exclaims the Princess to her friends. "I am so glad you found this place for me, or, good heavens, how ever would I have survived in that Forest all alone!" The animals nod and bow.

"Of course, I really must continue my journey to the Far Kingdom, where I will be completely safe. But I'm sure a couple of nights in this Cottage can't hurt, can they? I mean, those Magic Dildos are quite the bonus, aren't they?" she giggles. "Shame they disappear at dawn – or I am q uite sure I would spend the whole day getting fucked, as well as all night!" She yawns. "Oh see – I am q uite worn out! And won't it be jolly when I'm no longer a virgin, and they can fuck my cunt as well!" She giggles, and her friends laugh and gambol about sympathetically. "I do declare, though, it's going to be jolly difficult finding a Prince to merry out here in the woods, so I suppose I'll just have to get used to sticking large objects up my bottom instead, until I make it to the Far – ohhh!!!"

Snow White stops in shock, for suddenly, outside her window, there appears an unknown woman, tall, dark-haired, with a stern but handsome air, wearing a long black cloak and carrying a large wicker panier. "Good morning, fair maid," intones the woman in a deep velvety voice.

"Oh!" gasps the Princess. "Who are you? I didn't know anyone else lived out here in the woods – apart from the Seven Dildos, of course. Are you one of their friends...?" She notices that all her animal friends seem to have suddenly disappeared – but thinks nothing of it.

"I am a Magician," says the woman, her voice deep and seductive, "a Sorceress wishing to share my pleasure-bringing magic with you poor and painful peasantry. See what beauteous wares I can offer you!" She removes the checked cloth covering her basket to reveal a gleaming pile of fresh fruit: apples, bananas, peaches, plums, and deep red raspberries glistening with morning dew. "Would you like some?" she leers.

"Oh, they do look lovely," smiles Snow White. "But you know, I am hardly 'poor and painful': I am a Princess on the run, actually. And I never carry silver or gold; I rely on my court minions to provide such things – and there aren't any of them here now. So I couldn't possibly pay you," she explains earnestly.

"What's more, this house belongs to the Seven Dildos – and they only come out at night…"

"Oh, that is no obstacle," chuckles the woman warmly. "I am happy to let you try some of my magic wares free of charge. See, for example, this plum: doesn't it look delicious?" She waves the fruit before Show White's eyes and, indeed, it does seem irresistible: soft, juicy, gleaming, with an intoxicating perfume which fills the Princess' nostrils and sends her head reeling.

"Ohhhh," moans Snow White, "that smells jolly nice!" Instinctively, she parts her soft red lips, allowing the Sorceress to reach in through the kitchen window and gently stroke them with the deep purple surface of the plum. Her mouth begins to water, and the growing dampness on her lips makes the plum gleam and glisten yet more. The Sorceress applies gentle pressure to the enchanted fruit, and deep red juice flows onto Snow White's lips, dribbling down her chin.

"Oh, I say," pants Snow White. "That is utterly divine!" She extends her tongue, parting her lips to sq ueeze harder, so that the whole fruit bursts and smears over her lips, mouth and chin, juice dripping onto her dress. "Oh, but what a mess I have made of my clothes. And I've no lady-in-waiting here to clean it for me! Whatever shall I do?"

"Never mind your dress," intones the Sorceress.

"Leave it where it falls, and come out here to me," she chants. Her voice echoes in Snow White's head: "After all, wouldn't you like some more ... more ... more...?"

A loud series of knocks wakens Callum from his post-onanic reverie. "Come in!" he calls, hastily stuffing his softening penis back into his trousers – only to find his cabin door flung open to reveal a detachment of guards, led by none other than the Captain of the Palace Guard Sir John de Thomas. "Captain, Sir!" he exclaims, standing to attention and saluting. His fly is still unbuttoned.

"I am sorry, Callum," frowns the Captain, his eyes darting briefly from the open fly down to the freshly soiled deerskin rug and back to the Huntman's face, "but I am under orders from the Queen to arrest you, on charges of attempting to deceive the Crown. You must come with me at once, to the Dungeons."

Snow White stands naked on the grass before the Cottage of the Seven Dildos, plum juice smeared on her face and dripping off her chin onto her full breasts. "Oh, truly you are beautiful, Princess," pants the Sorceress under her breath. "The Mirror was right."

"Mirror?" asks Snow White, bewildered and disorientated, as she feels her lips and nipples tingle with desire.

The Sorceress waves the q uestion away with her hand. "Never mind!" she chuckles, her deep voice burrowing into Snow White's consciousness. "Look instead at this!" She holds up a peach: glowing in the sunlight, its scent is rich, sweet and powerful – and the Princess wants it, desires it, needs it.

"Give it me!" trembles Snow White, parting her lips wide even as she reaches for the soft fruit with her hand. The Sorceress lets the ripe peach drop into Snow White's delicate pale palm. The Princess squeezes it, feels the juice run down her arm, then plasters it over her face and breasts, before reaching down to rub the soft yellow flesh into her vulva. "Good Lord!" she cries, as unalloyed pleasure takes hold of her whole being, "Gratias agimus tibi propter labia maiora tua!" she sq ueals, pressing peach-flesh into her tits and cunt and collapsing to her knees in magical ecstasy.

The Sorceress laughs with delight. She casts her cloak off to reveal her naked body – hair black, skin pale, lips red as the rose, but still magically unrecognisable by the Princess. Her breasts are full on her slender body – but the girl's attention is drawn to the long, thick, stiff penis now bulging from the Sorceress' crotch: throbbing, tumescent, powerful. "O Sorceress, O Magician," she gasps, pointing to the magic futa-cock, already dripping with translucent pre-cum, "I didn't know that you could … you could … ohhh…" Snow White's sentence disintegrates into a moan of desire as, continuing to rub her nectar-sweetened clit and paw at her own fruit-spattered breasts, she shuffles forward on her knees, lips parted, tongue drooling.

The Magician grabs a handful of raspberries from her magic basket and squeezes them over her thick shaft, so that her whole cock is now dripping with sweet red enchanted juice. She reaches for the back of Snow White's head and urges it forward questioningly.

Snow White nods and opens her mouth wider in affirmation, allowing the Sorceress's fragrant dripping shaft to power its way into her throat. "Aaaarggh!" gags the Princess, as the huge cock begins a slow but deep throatfuck, eliciting ropes of berry-coloured saliva from the girl's desperate mouth.

The metal gate clangs shut, and Callum the Huntsman collapses on the floor of his cell in despair. Sir John de Thomas turns the key in the lock but, instead of departing swiftly as he should, pauses awhile, as if struggling with whether to speak or not.

"I'm so sorry, Callum," he says eventually.

Callum looks up. "Am I to be executed, Sir John?" he asks.

Sir John nods. "The Queen has ordered it for dawn tomorrow."

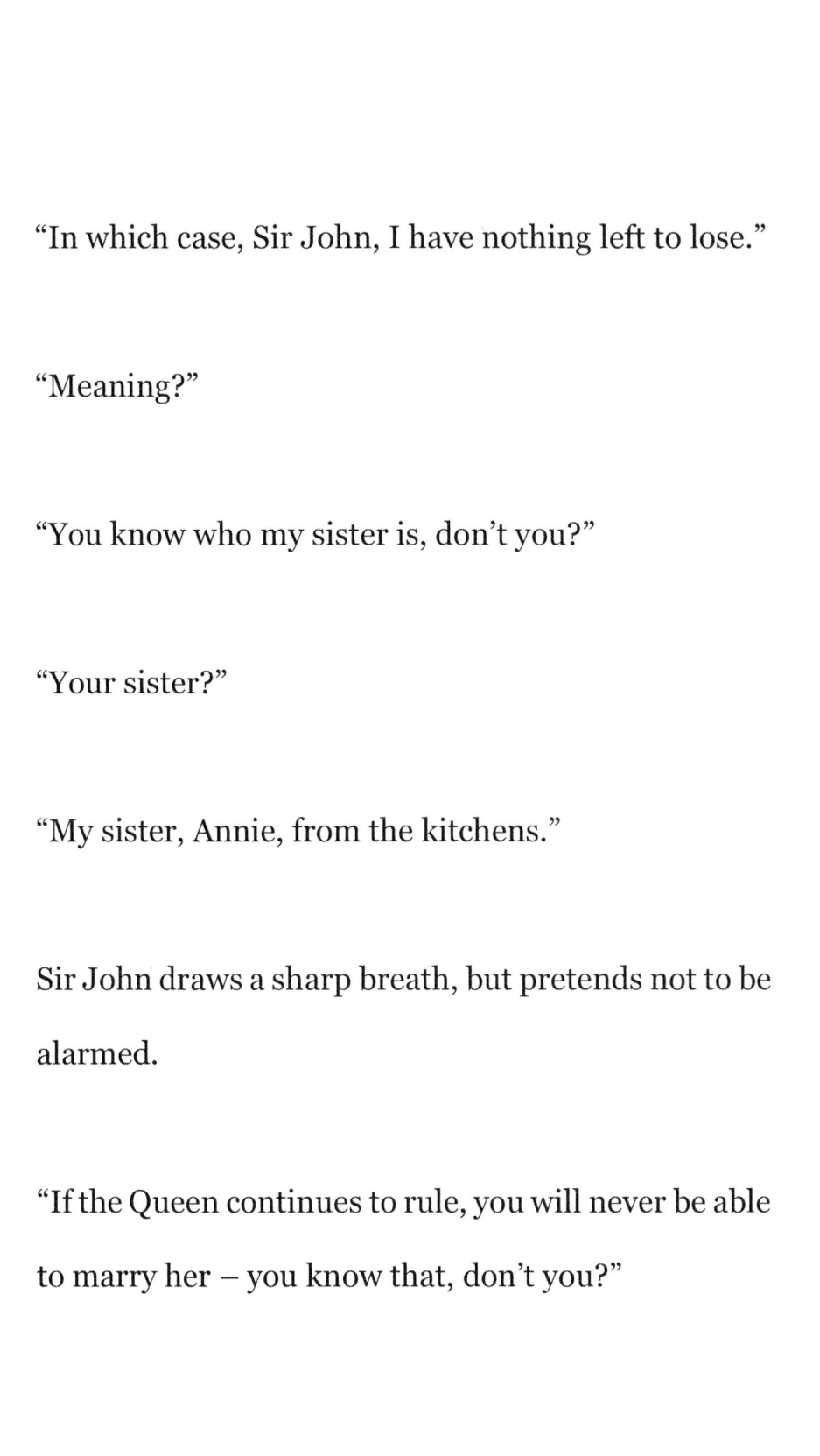

"In which case, Sir John, I have nothing left to lose."

"Meaning?"

"You know who my sister is, don't you?"

"Your sister?"

"My sister, Annie, from the kitchens."

Sir John draws a sharp breath, but pretends not to be alarmed.

"If the Queen continues to rule, you will never be able to marry her – you know that, don't you?"

Sir John sets his jaw. "I don't know what you mean," he lies.

"Fine, Captain. You can pretend if you like. But I don't have to pretend any more, do I? I know how much you despise the Queen in your heart. And I say there is a way out. Snow White has fled to the Far Kingdom. There are many other exiles there. We could join her, you and I, and raise an army. This Land could be set free again."

Sir John shakes his head grimly. "No, Callum, Snow White has not reached the Far Kingdom. She is staying in the Cottage of the Seven Dildos, in the Great Forest."

"What?! How came you by this information?"

"The Queen's Mirror has revealed it. That is how Her Majesty knew you had betrayed her trust. She is on her way to the Cottage as we speak, to work some of her accursed Magic on the Princess. Snow White is doomed."

"Oh God!" cries the Huntsman in horror. "You must let me go, Sir John, I beg of you!" Desperately, he rattles the bars of his cell.

"How can I do that, Callum? Would you wish the vengeance of the Queen on me too?"

"If I manage to save Snow White, and the Queen is defeated, then there may be peace and justice in the Land again," says the Huntsman urgently. And then he adds, "And you might marry my sister."

Callum sees a glimmer of hope pass swiftly across Sir John's face – before being rapidly effaced by a frown, then a sigh. The Captain says nothing.

"Please, Sir John," continues the Huntsman. "No one need know. I have only one desire, and that is to save the Princess. You have nothing to lose – and possibly everything to gain. Please."

Kneeling on the lawn before the Cottage of the Seven Dildos, Snow White is in enchanted ecstasy – but the

Queen is in control. "Oh yes, my filthy cock-sucking, fruit-fucking Princess," she pants, as she continues to fuck Snow White's face, "you want more, don't you? TELL ME!" she bellows.

"Mooore!" moans the Princess through her throatful of magic fruit and pounding cock.

The Queen reaches for a banana – thick, glowing, glistening, irresistible. She peels it, allowing its heady magical scent to reach the Princess's nostrils, even as she continues to be face-fucked by her pounding futa-cock. "In your cunt, Princess?!" she asks.

"Nooooo!" glubs the Princess. "My 'unt i' for my Pwince awone! Pu' i' in my aaar–ghhh!!"

Snow White lies back on the soft grass, roughly pulling the Queen on top of her into a sixty-nine. The Sorceress continues to pound her girlcock in and out of the Princess' fruit-smeared face, whilst reaching down and squelching the full length of the peeled banana into her gaped anus. "OH JOLLY FUCKING HOCKEYSTICKS!" squeals Snow White, as an exquisite magical banana-induced pleasure grips her anus. She expels the Queen's cock from her mouth as she screams, "MOTHERFUCKING MARVELLOUS, EH WHAT! NOW MOOOOORE!!!"

Callum the Huntsman is riding. Through the Great Forest he gallops, eastwards in pursuit of the Princess, in search of the Cottage of the Seven Dildos.

Over hills and through dales, he fords streams, vaults over rocky outcrops – till he comes to a place deep in the Forest where the road forks.

"Damn!" he curses, rearing his horse. "Which way is it?" He wavers for a few minutes, desperate to remember. But it is then that he hears a noise of galloping approaching along one of the side paths. He freezes in alarm – until round a bend in the path charges a company of animals: two deer, each bearing on its back a small bevy of sq uirrels and rabbits – and a turtle. "Where is she?" he calls. "Take me to her!"

The animals turn and gallop away down the right-hand fork. Callum follows.

"MORE?!" shouts the Queen, as she kneels on the ground between Snow White's thighs. "What about this, my beauteous Princess whore?!" She retrieves a deep red apple from her panier. "Can you take this in your royal fucking shithole?"

"OH YES, YES, YES!" screams Snow White. She reaches down, lifts her buttocks, and pulls her banana-smeared anus open with three fingers of each hand, so that her pulsating rectum gapes apple-wide. "PUT THAT APPLE IN MY ARSEHOLE, O MOTHERFUCKING MAGICIAN!"

"YES! YES!! YES!!!" screams the Queen. She brandishes her gleaming magic apple, and rams it into Snow White's arsehole in one brutal thrust, before screeching, "NOW I WILL BE THE FAIREST IN THE LAND!!!"

"What?!" mutters Snow White in bewilderment. She feels the stretch of her anus, now gaped wider than ever before by a magic apple, crowned gloriously at her quivering entrance. There is pleasure, there is pain, there is triumph, there is the ecstasy of feeling her dirt-orifice stretched wide. But now also there is confusion: "Fairest in the...?"

And then the Princess notices something different: where her stretched-out arsehole has been tingling and throbbing at the touch and penetration of magic fruit, now something quite new and strange is happening. The sensations fade – and she cannot feel anything there anymore. The numbness spreads, and now she can no longer feel her cunt, nor her thighs. She tries to move her legs – but cannot even sense their presence.

She looks up and, to her horror, recognises, not an unknown Sorceress, but the Queen, her Queen, her Stepmother, kneeling between her thighs, gloating triumphantly. "Your Majesty?" she asks, dazed and confused, as the magic ecstasy of plum, peach, raspberry and banana continues to fade, leaving anaesthesia and lethargy in its wake, gradually spreading up her body. In desperation, she paws at her breasts – but cannot feel them either. Panic grips her, as she begins to feel her consciousness fading.

"What is happening?" she cries.

Melancholy overtakes Snow White, and her life begins to pass before her eyes: times long gone, when all was happiness and light, and life was full of kindness and joy, and everything shimmered with meaning and promise. She remembers her childhood, playing in the Palace grounds while her loving widowed Father looked on indulgently. She remembers the Queen, her Stepmother, once so charming and elegant as her Father fell in love with her, her eyes glinting with satisfaction as they exchanged vows. And then, her Stepmother's concealed triumphant grin as she stood by her husband's bedside watching him gasp his last breath, victim of what all the court physicians could only describe as "a mysterious disease". The Queen sports the same evil grin now, as she stands to gloat over her second royal victim. "Oh God!" whimpers Snow White. "Father ... I miss you so much ... Help me ... Help me..."

"No one can help you now," pants the Queen, who is now hand-pumping her huge girlcock with unalloyed power-lust. "Your fool of a Father could not withstand my magic – and nor will you!" She cackles dementedly, rolling her eyes in ecstasy as her huge cock explodes in triumph, releasing stream after stream of hot futa-cum over the twitching body of the Princess, decorating her face, lips, tits and cunt with cock-slime, garnishing the multi-coloured melange of juice and fruit-flesh already adorning her pale skin. She aims her last three thick spurts of cum across the red apple still crowning Snow White's gaped anus. Futa-semen drips down the surface of the fruit, across Snow White's anal rim, and onto the soft green grass.

"FUCK YOU, SNOW WHITE!" cackles the Queen, throwing back her head to scream her victory to the skies, as Snow White moans helplessly, and her eyes flutter shut.

But she is not alone anymore. "HALT, O QUEEN!" cries a voice, as Callum the Huntsman and his forest menagerie come galloping into the clearing before the Cottage. He charges towards her, brandishing his axe. But the Queen holds up the palm of one hand

and utters a foul magical incantation: an invisible enchanted missile issues forth and knocks the Huntsman off his horse and onto the ground.

"TOO LATE, MY TREACHEROUS HUNTSMAN!" roars the Queen. "Snow White will never wake again! For only True Love's Arsefuck can break this spell — and no man has ever been capable of that! From now on, I AM THE FAIREST OF THEM ALL!" She laughs again, a hideous triumphant evil cackle which echoes throughout the Forest — before whirling around and, in a burst of flame and wind, disappearing.

Snow White lies immobile on the ground, her body adorned with peach flesh, plum and raspberry juice, mashed banana, and Sorceress-cum, the magic apple lodged brutally in her anus. Callum kneels before her and weeps. And the forest animals gather round, wailing and keening their broken hearts to the wind.

CHAPTER 5

The Huntsman kneels by Snow White's body and weeps. "O God!" he cries. "Why could I not save her? O my beloved Snow White!"

Tears running unstaunched down his cheeks, he carefully lifts Snow White's naked sleeping body and carries it down to the stream, where he washes her from head to foot, gently rinsing the magic fruit juices and futa-cum out of her hair and off her skin, pulling the accursed apple out of her arsehole with a soft sq uelch and burning it, burying the ashes beneath a thick stone slab. The animals pat the Princess' skin dry with leaves and moss, braiding her hair with wildflowers, so that she looks as beautiful in sleep as in wakefulness, whilst the Huntsman finds some logs with which to construct a low bier onto which to lay her precious body.

"Only True Love's Arsefuck the spell shall break," whispers the Huntsman – and so he lies Snow White on her front on the bier, knees tucked below her, bottom raised slightly upwards on a cushion of moss, leaves and flowers, so that her now tight exposed pucker smiles at the azure sky, ready for the arrival of whosoever might try to penetrate it – and break the curse.

It must be a Prince, thinks the Huntsman. That is what she would want.

And so he prepares a parchment, writing on it in tall bold letters:

The Princess Snow White is before the Cottage of the Seven Dildos in the Great Forest, locked into a Magical Slumber which may only be broken by True Love's Arsefuck. Let any Prince in the Kingdom or Beyond approach with Love, to wake the Princess from her Curse.

"Take this," he says to Snow White's animal friends, "and have the finest scribes in the Land and Beyond make copies, and let them be sent to All the Ends of the Earth – that the greatest Princes in the Whole World may come and prove their Love for Snow White!"

And so the weeks pass. By day, the animals keep watch over Snow White's body, washing and grooming her, renewing the flowers in her hair, bathing her skin in fragrant oils and perfumes, so that she remains fair as ever, her tight anus pristine, expectant and glistening. The deer stand guard, the birds sing lullabies to their sweet slumbering friend, the rabbits and squirrels tidy and trim the lawn, and the turtle just sits and watches. The Seven Dildos take the night shift, their shafts vertical, their heads pulsating with magical luminescence, casting an eerie but dignified light over the Princess' body. And in the corner, under the eaves of the Cottage, sits Callum the Huntsman, ever weeping and mourning his lost Princess.

And so the months pass. Princes come and go, trying their luck at waking Snow White. The first is the Prince of the North, dressed in a coat of reindeer skins, with thick fur boots – despite it being the middle of summer. Tall and rugged, with short blond hair, he wears a gauntlet of woven gold. His penis is large, thick and pale, and it stands to attention as soon as he approaches Snow White's bier and spies the beauty of her perfumed lubricated arsehole glistening at him from between her pale buttocks. "Hot fucking arsehole," he mutters. "Dirty fucking shit-bitch: all you need is a good hard cock to ream that filthy shitter – don't you?" He sniggers callously under his breath.

Callum stands. "Insult not my mistress!" he cries, his voice trembling and indignant.

"'Insult not'?" laughs the Prince. "She's nothing but a cheap anal whore – kneeling there with her arsehole exposed for anyone to come and fuck, ha!" He climbs onto the bier, cock gripped firmly in his hands, ready to plunge it mercilessly into the Princess' anus. But the moment his cock approaches within an inch of Snow White's arse-crack, a magical force envelops the Princess' body, casting the Prince up into the air and hurling him fifty yards across the clearing, where he lands in a crumpled heap against a gnarled birch tree. He curses in pain and humiliation before limping away, never to be seen again.

The second Prince to arrive, as falling leaves usher in an early autumn, is the Prince of the East – slender and precious, his dark hair tied back in a ponytail and a curled moustache gracing his upper lip. Long silver robes trail along the ground behind him, and multicoloured gemstones shine on his fingers. His cock is long and thin, and it too goes erect at the first sight of Snow White's anal beauty. He thinks – but does not say out loud – for he is a wily fellow: You could make me rich and powerful, Princess. Our Kingdoms joined could rule the World. And with your arse to fuck every night, every Pleasure would be mine!

Callum does not trust him, but has been given no reason to issue any challenge. Instead he watches suspiciously as the Prince aims his cock at Snow White's tight pucker and lunges. However, the moment his shaft approaches within an inch of her, he too is magically thrown back. His body whirls several times head over heels in mid-air, before landing with an almighty splash in the stream.

The Prince of the South is next to arrive. By now it is cold, and a thin layer of snow lies on the ground. Snow White's body, however, remains warm, protected in its magical slumber, and a soft mist rises from her pale exposed buttocks. Despite the weather, this Prince is bare-chested, with a leopard-skin cape over his back. Shards of shells and bones pierce his nose, ears and nipples, and the shaft of his huge black cock is pierced by a thick whale-bone peg. He laughs as soon as he sees Snow White – a loud laugh of mockery and scorn as he surveys the girl whom he has chosen to own. He pumps his cock into a huge erection and stands above the Princess. "MY FUCK-SLAVE!" he roars, as he aims at her arsehole – but screams in rage as he too is cast into the air and across the lawn, landing with a loud thump against the outer wall of the Cottage.

Callum looks down at him with scorn, and spits onto the ground.

And so it continues, month after month. Every few weeks a new Prince arrives, only to be magically cast aside as he attempts to sodomise the Princess. "True Love," sighs Callum to himself again and again. "Will no Prince approach my Mistress with Love in 'is 'eart?"

Now it is spring again – nearly a year since the Princess was cursed, and still the animals, the Seven Dildos, and the Huntsman keep watch over her beloved sleeping body. Callum goes over in his mind, again and again, the words of the evil Queen, and of Snow White before her:

... only True Love's Arsefuck can break this spell...

... I really ought to marry a Prince, not a 'Cuntsman'...

... but I swear to you, my Royal Cuntsman, that the next time we meet, you may fuck the Royal Arse...

And he ponders. And he dreams. And he wonders whether he loves Snow White enough. He is no prince, though – aye, there's the rub ... But, he thinks, even if I may never marry 'er, God knows 'ow much I adore 'er... True Love's Arsefuck ... Is this True Love? Will I ever know?

Well, there is one way to know, ponders the Huntsman. If I am cast away by magic and break a bone or two – well, no great matter. But if it wake the Princess and save the Kingdom, then surely it will have been worthwhile, even if she turn 'er back on me after.

"Snow White," he whispers under his breath. "from

the day I first remember ye playing in the Palace gardens, you 'ave been the light of my life, you 'ave been my greatest joy. And though I be banished or executed for the perfidy of it, I can at least try this one thing, to bring your light back into the world. For what I am about to do, Snow White, I beg you to forgive me. For I do this not to possess you, but to free you..."

It is night. The animals are asleep, and the soft rainbow glow of the Seven Dildos standing guard shines over the sleeping Princess. Callum removes his clothes, walks over to the bier, bows respectfully to Snow White's mooning buttocks, and climbs up.

Snow White is beautiful. He cannot see her face, but

her bottom shines pale in the silver light of the full moon, reflecting the kaleidoscope of soft colours emanating from the Seven pulsating Dildos. Her anus, tight as a starfish, but glistening and fragrant with the oils of flowers and herbs with which the animals have dressed it, shines with unfathomable allure. The Huntsman smiles. "Snow White, you are beautiful!" he mutters. The Dildos appear to nod in affirmation.

Callum kneels next to the sleeping Princess, reaches out, and gently touches her back. It is warm to the touch, and he can sense her body slowly rising and falling with her breath. He runs his hand softly up and down her naked back, feels the gentle undulation of her smooth flesh beneath his fingers. His hand finds the crease of her buttocks, and he gently strokes one finger down into the soft valley of her bottom. It is warmer still there, and slightly moist, and he can smell the sweet sweaty scent of her fundament wafting upwards towards him. Carefully he leans over and kisses one buttock. It jiggles slightly, and the warm fragrance of the Princess' anus rises even more richly to his nostrils.

"O Snow White!" he cries again. "May you someday find your Prince, to whom to give your vaginal virginity, to marry, and with whom to rule this Kingdom in truth and goodness." He kisses both her buttocks now, then buries his face between them, to gently touch his lips to her anus. It is pursed, like a little mouth, creased but soft, its rich scent throwing him into joyous ecstasy. His penis begins to harden and, from where he is, gently brushes against the Princess's calves.

Callum kisses down the backs of Snow White's thighs, past her knees, till he finds her feet. Carefully lifting her calves upwards so he can kiss her toes, he sucks each one in turn, swirling his tongue around to taste the goodness of her flesh. His tongue traces its way back up her legs until it finds the crack of her bottom again. He can smell her vulva too, sweet and rich, but he deliberately ignores it (That's for the Prince!) to delve his tongue back into her arse-crack. Now he is licking and probing and slobbering with joyous abandon, feeling his penis reach full strength in appreciation, as the Princess' anus begins to soften and loosen further. Soon it opens slightly to the tip of his tongue, which he slips into the space within her winking rim, to begin a slow anal tongue-fuck.

He remembers her words:

... the next time we meet, you may fuck the Royal Arse...

"Fuck the Royal Arse," he mutters. "God 'elp me." He pulls Snow White's legs gently apart and kneels between her thighs, his rigid cock poised at her brown hole. Gently he touches his glans to her now winking pucker. To his relief, he is not magically blasted back, but feels the first drop of his pre-cum lubricate the Princess' soft yielding flesh. He leans forward and pushes gently.

In her Palace, the Queen is in ecstasy. "Oh yes, my Foul Fucking Fenestration, let me bathe in thy cum, let me feel thy Servile Slime all over my body," she moans. She has been eaten out, rimmed, fingered and fucked by her Magic Mirror, and cum adorns her face and hair, dribbles off her chin and tits, squelches into her cunt and arsehole, and forms a pungent puddle all over the floor. She crouches to slurp the gloop up off the cool marble, so she can swill it around in her mouth, savour the taste, gargle with it, and let it drool sluttishly from her mouth. She blows bubbles, letting them splatter over her face, muttering satisfied obscenities under her breath.

"Fo, am I ftill the Fairwest in the Wand, my Magic Miwt Miwwaaargh?" glubs the Queen through a throatful of fuck-slime. It is a rhetorical q uestion, of course, for the response has been the same every day for the past year. But she loves to hear the answer, adores basking in the self-adulation it affords her. She awaits the Mirror's customary affirmation, fingers poised to rub her clit again in confirmatory narcissistic self-pleasure.

But this time the Mirror's response alarms her: "Fair art thou, O Quimly Queen, whether pristine or Covered in Cum. But just one more proof I need to confirm thy Pre-eminent Pulchritude. Turn and face me again, O Whoring Highness, that I may douse thy face with my Windowpane Wee, wash my gloop off your Beauteous Body with my Pungent Piss, see thee drowned in Number One!"

"What?" trembles the Queen. "Is that truly necessary, O Wanking Windowglass?"

"If thou wouldst know that verily thou art the Fairest in the Land, then it must be done, O Queen," intones the Mirror solemnly.

In bewilderment and confusion, the Queen kneels.

Callum feels the full length of his cock slowly slide into the Princess' rectum. "Oh," he whimpers, as bliss overtakes him.

"Ohhh..." moans another voice. "Is that you, Callum the Cuntsman?"

"Princess? Princess Snow White?" Callum's voice trembles. "What, awake? Is the spell broken then?"

"Oh, I'm terribly glad it's you, Master Callum," squeaks Snow White. "What took you so long? I did say you could fuck the Royal Arse, didn't I? And those Princes were such a bunch of deadbeats: I'd much rather be fucked by you!"

Callum the Cuntsman laughs – a great peal of laughter, full of joy and relief, which makes his cock jiggle in the depths of his lover's rectum. He feels Snow White push upwards against him, drawing him even deeper into her, so that his testicles slap against her damp vulva. "Go on then, Master Cuntsman, pound that Royal Arse! Or need I do my ridiculous West Country impression again?" Snow White giggles.

"Yer Majesty may do as she pleases!" chuckles the Hunstman, as he begins to slide his cock in and out of the Royal Rectum, feeling it squeeze him tight as he fucks his beloved mistress.

"I should jolly well think so!" laughs the Princess. "And so I think I will stick to my own accent, if that's all right with you. After all, if I'm going to merry you I will have to keep up some standards, won't I?"

Callum freezes, his cock buried halfway into his mistress' rectum. "Wha-at?" he stutters in shock. "Marry me?"

"Well, otherwise how ever are you going to take my vaginal virginity, young man?"

"But ... I thought that was only for a Prince!" replies Callum, his cock still stuck Excalibur-like in the Royal Arsehole. In his astonishment, he has stopped fucking.

"Oh yes, I quite forgot! Quick, on your knees, spit spot!" Snow White pushes Callum out of her anus and off the bier, and gestures for him to kneel at her feet. "Now, where's that ridiculous axe of yours?" (Of course, she pronounces it "ex" – as a Princess should.) "Ah!" she spies it leaning against the wall of the Cottage, walks over, and drags it back to her kneeling Huntsman, whose cock remains stiff with desire despite his bewilderment. Summoning all her strength, she lifts the axe high above her head before swinging it downwards towards Callum. The Huntsman screams in terror – but the Princess, stronger than she looks, halts the weapon just above his shoulder, giggles, and rests it there, before declaiming in her most solemn tones, "I dub thee Prince Callum the Cuntsman, Royal Consort! Now arise, Prince Cuntsman, and fuck me!!!" She drops the axe, and opens her arms wide with glee.

The Queen is kneeling on the marble floor before her

Mirror, her hands clasped behind her back, eyes shut tight, face upturned, mouth open wide.

"Take this, Palace Pisswhore," sneers the Mirror, before the Queen feels a thick stream of Pungent Pee stream into her mouth. She chokes and spits out the golden liquid – but it continues to flow, streaming over her face, hair and tits, washing her body clean of semen. A foul melange of piss and cum courses down her skin and onto the floor, leaving her crouched, humiliated and stinking of asparagus, her skin steaming with fresh urine.

The Queen holds back her tears, repeating boldly, though through trembling lips, "Am I the Fairest of Them All, O Mirror? Say it now!"

There is a long pause, before the Mirror speaks: "Fair art thou, O Queen, and thy lips are red as the rose, thy skin as white as snow, thy hair black as ebony; thy tits as Fulsomely Fuckable, thy Courtly Cunt as tight and pink, thy August Arsehole as Pungently Perfect as any in the Land. Thou art indeed fair, whether immaculate of air, or even covered with cum and piss. But behold – Snow White has awoken, roused from slumber by Callum the Royal Huntsman, by the power of True Love's Arsefuck. She is again the Fairest in the Land!"

"WHAT?!" screams the Queen. "Betrayed again?!! GUAAARDS!!!"

The guards come running, led by their Captain Sir John de Thomas. They screech to a halt at the threshold, as they see their Queen crouched on the floor in the middle of a foul pond, reeking of piss and cum. "WHAT ARE YOU WAITING FOR?" she screeches. "Snow White has been awoken by the Royal Huntsman! I want them both dead! Into the Forest, all of you, and bring their filthy heads to me on a platter! NOW!!!"

But Sir John pauses, as he realises what has happened. He remembers Callum's plea for help a year ago. He recalls his own failure at the time: tractable enough to quietly let the Huntsman go free, yet too cowardly to offer assistance to his quest. He thinks of his secret beloved Annie, and realises again that, if the benevolent Snow White were on the throne, he could marry her. He feels ashamed at his own small-mindedness, his lack of ambition and principle. And then he looks down at his Queen, pathetically crawling through her stinking puddle, sploshing and glubbing through cum and piss, now pawing at his foot: "Sir Thomas, I want her dead. Go, bwing me my step-daughter's head. Because I want to be the Fairwest in the Whole Fucking Wand! I want to be pwetty! I want to be beautiful! I want it! Want it! Want it!"

The scales fall from Sir John's eyes, and he realises the illusory futility of his position, recognises his own cowardice, sees how he has collaborated with evil all these years. He looks with distaste at the pathetic excuse of a Queen wriggling before him, imagines again what could instead be, if justice and truth were restored to the Land. Now his decision is made: he raises his sword, and brings it down in one mighty swoop; its task is accomplished in a stroke.

Meanwhile, Snow White is lying on her back on the soft grass before the Cottage of the Seven Dildos. Callum the Cuntsman is poised above her, his hard cockhead gently nudging at her vulva. She spreads her outer lips with her fingers to expose her intact hymen, stretched and inviting, whilst intoning with ecclesiastical solemnity:

Gratias agimus tibi propter labia maiora tua!

Callum's cock ruptures Snow White's hymen in one mighty swoop; its task too is accomplished in a stroke.

And so Snow White and her Cuntsman fuck, and fuck, and fuck. Sometimes his cock plunges in and out of her tight wet cunt, sometimes nestles deep in her magnificently gaping arsehole, sometimes slides back and forth between her bulging breasts, sometimes explores the depths of her dribbling throat. With exultant abandon he sucks her fulsome tits, he eats her hot pink pussy, his tongue curling and scooping so as to revel in the glorious tang of her deep-cunt slime, before slithering downwards to flick and probe again at her pungent anus. She in turn sucks his cock, sometimes sliding down to lick his heavy balls whilst her delicate palm strokes his throbbing shaft, before burying her beautiful royal visage between the Huntsman's buttocks to taste his hairy rim. And they both come again and again and again, their bodies rolling and lunging and embracing with joy, their juices mixing and melding as they laugh and whoop and proclaim their shared ecstasy to the world.

Throughout, the Seven Dildos maintain their guard of honour, their soft kaleidoscope of colours illuminating the scene unfolding before them. They do not interfere or join in – for, though lustful in inclination, and desirous as any would be of the fragrant depths of the Princess' orifices, they are nevertheless wise Dildos, and know to rein in their concupiscence, to honour others' True Love.

As dawn breaks over the clearing, the Dildos end their vigil and disappear, and the animals wake up, to chirrup and gambol with delight at their Princess' awakening. Then Snow White and her Huntsman pause their fucking for a while, and she says, "Prince Callum the Cuntsman, will you marry me?"

Of course, she pronounces it a bit like "merry me" – as a true Princess should.

And of course, Callum says yes.

There is great rejoicing in the Land at the news of the evil Queen's death, and the rightful accession of the new Queen Snow White. She is crowned in the Abbey amid great pomp and circumstance, before she and Prince Callum are married.

Freed from the shackles of the old regime, Sir John de Thomas and Annie the scullery maid are also wed. Prince Callum acts as Best Man, and Snow White – in a breach of courtly etiquette, to be sure, but to great popular acclaim – is her Chief Bridesmaid. No one notices, though, when Snow White leans forward and whispers into Annie's ear, "Is 'e goin' to fuck yer arrse tonoight, Annie?"

Annie giggles.

And They All Live Happily Ever After.

AUTHOR NOTE

Thank you for reading this story, I hope you enjoyed it as much as i did writing it for you. The concluding part of the story will be in the next edition of this book attached to it as a series, hopefully, it would have been released by the time you are reading this. I will really love your feedback so i will have my eyes on my email inbox, so, therefore, please kindly use the comment section of where you purchased this book from to place your reviews, suggestion and ratings for this book for it will help me improve the forth coming stories that are yet to be released.

You can contact me the author via my email (viaoptimisticdaily@gmail.com).

Printed in Great Britain
by Amazon